The Adventures of Sam X

THE STATUE'S SECRET

by Hubert Ben Kemoun

illustrated by Thomas Ehretsmann

translated by Genevieve Chamberland

STONE ARCH BOOKS
www.stonearchbooks.com

First published in the United States in 2009
by Stone Arch Books,
151 Good Counsel Drive, P.O. Box 669
Mankato, Minnesota 56002
www.stonearchbooks.com

Library of Congress Cataloging-in-Publication Data
Ben Kemoun, Hubert, 1958–
    [Retour d'Archibald. English]
    The Statue's Secret / by Hubert Ben Kemoun; illustrated by Thomas
Ehretsmann.
    p. cm. — (Pathway Books Editions. The Adventures of Sam X)
    Originally published: Le retour d'Archibal. France: Nathan, 2007.
    ISBN 978-1-4342-1220-7 (library binding)
    [1. Statues—Fiction. 2. Supernatural—Fiction.] I. Ehretsmann, Thomas,
ill. II. Title.
PZ7.B4248St 2009
[Fic]—dc22   2008031579

Summary: Sam and his friend Lionel discover something incredible in the
river — a walking, talking statue named Archibald. The statue asks the
boys for help to find his way to the city. The result is an incredible journey
full of helpful gargoyles, frozen bullies, and eventually, the reunion of two
long-lost stone friends.

Creative Director: Heather Kindseth
Graphic Designer: Emily Harris

1 2 3 4 5 6 14 13 12 11 10 09

Printed in the United States of America

TABLE OF CONTENTS

Chapter 1

LIONEL'S FEET

"My feet hurt so much," Lionel said, looking down at his bare feet. "They are covered in blisters. I think I walked on every street of the whole city today."

I held my nose and replied, "With your stinky feet, you could empty out the whole city!"

Lionel looked at me.

"They have to breathe!" he said. He rubbed his toes.

"Okay," I said, "but is that a reason to make everyone else suffer?"

Lionel shrugged. "They don't smell that bad," he said.

There was no point arguing with him. Nothing could have changed Lionel's good mood that afternoon. He had been in a good mood ever since we started out on our walk along the river, taking pictures.

Lionel loved springtime. He loved the blossoms, the sparkling river, and the fresh spring air.

He thought everything was wonderful. If a tornado had headed for us, I think he would have said, "This is great!" before finding a place to hide from the storm.

My friend was floating on a cloud of happiness, and I knew why. It was because of his new digital camera. His parents had given it to him for his birthday.

I could see why Lionel was so happy. It really was a great camera. It was the nicest one I'd ever seen.

So we had agreed to try it out near the river that afternoon.

Lionel said that his feet hurt too much to keep going, so we were taking a break by the river. But I was tired of resting.

Lionel decided to save the planet by putting his shoes back on. Then we got up and started walking again.

We were on a little beach that was covered with pebbles. There were some patches of grass and some trees nearby.

Suddenly, Lionel screamed and pointed at the shore. "Look!" he yelled. "Do you see it?"

"What?" I asked.

I looked where he was pointing. All I could see was sand, tall grass coming out of the gravel, and some twisted branches stuck in the river.

I didn't see anything worth yelling about. I didn't even see anything worth taking a picture of.

"What is the big deal, Lionel?" I asked.

Lionel was still pointing. He stepped backward and said, "Look! There's a zombie arm coming out of the water!"

His face was really pale. I had never seen him look so nervous.

I shook my head and laughed. "Are you nuts?" I said. "Some photographer you are. You can't even tell the difference between a fallen branch and a zombie arm."

I stepped forward to look more closely at the branch. Then I stopped talking. I looked again.

My heart started racing. My legs started shaking. I felt like an icy wind had just blown on me.

I thought it was a piece of wood, but I was wrong.

It was an arm. It was covered with a dirty piece of cloth, and it was pointing at the sky.

For a few minutes, I couldn't say anything. I couldn't look away from that arm, coming out of nowhere. Behind me, I could hear the click of Lionel's camera as he took as many pictures as he could.

Then I realized something. I turned around and said, "Lionel, it's not an arm. It's just part of a statue. Let's pull it out of the water. It's just an arm from a statue!"

I did not know yet that there was a shoulder, a chest, and a lot more at the other end of the statue's arm.

Chapter 2

THE STATUE SPEAKS

It took us fifteen minutes to dig up that little statue. It was heavy and hard to pick up. We laid it on a rock once we got it out of the river. Then we wiped off the mud.

The statue was of an old man with a big, bushy beard. It was about two feet tall. It was wearing a long cape and sandals. A hood covered its head and part of its face.

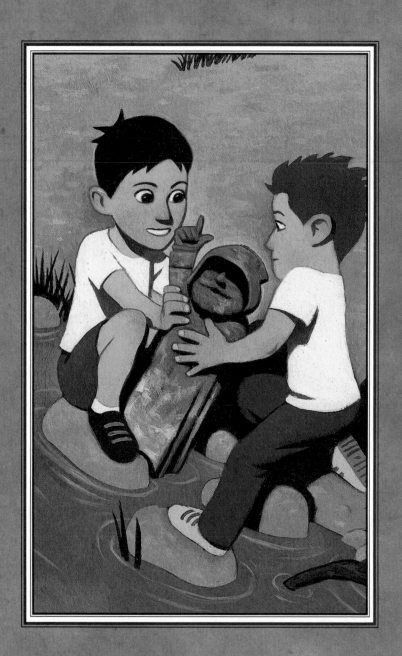

Lionel was so excited he could hardly sit still.

"We found a treasure!" he yelled. "A treasure! I bet they'll write a story about us in the newspaper, and they'll use the pictures I took! We'll be famous! Famous, Sam, famous!"

I shook my head. "Maybe, but first, we have to carry it to the police station or the museum. It weighs a lot. It will take us a really long time to carry this thing that far," I said.

"Then we should get started soon!" Lionel said.

He held out his camera and added, "First, take this. I want you to take a picture of me standing next to the statue."

I laughed. Earlier, Lionel wouldn't have let me use his camera if I paid him a million dollars. Now he wanted to have a photo shoot next to the statue.

I took four or five pictures of him with the river as a background.

Then, suddenly, I started to feel kind of weird. Kind of uncomfortable.

I wasn't sure why. I couldn't explain it.

Maybe I was just tired, or maybe it was because of a shadow or something, but suddenly it seemed like the statue's cape moved. But that was silly. I was just imagining things.

Lionel and I picked up the statue and started walking. Lionel had his camera strapped over his shoulder. He was holding the statue's head. I was behind him, holding the statue's feet.

At first, carrying the statue wasn't that bad. But then we started heading up a hill. All of a sudden, Lionel tripped on a tree root.

It all happened so fast. Lionel slid toward the tree to catch his balance. He didn't want to fall and let go of the statue.

Then the statue's right hand — the one that had been pointing at the sky — opened up!

I watched, amazed, as the statue reached up and grabbed a tree branch. It was helping! It didn't want Lionel to fall!

The statue only held on for a few seconds. Soon he let go of the branch, but that was enough for me. I was shocked. The statue had moved!

I dropped the statue's feet. "Lionel! It's not a statue!" I yelled. "Watch out!"

Lionel quickly dropped the front of the statue.

Our treasure fell onto the ground. Then it rolled back down the hill toward the river.

"You're crazy!" Lionel yelled. "Why did you say that? What's wrong with you?"

"Look!" I whispered. I pointed toward the statue, lying on the sand.

At first, the statue moved very slowly. He carefully found his balance on the ground.

Then the statue kneeled on the ground. He slowly stood up and looked at us.

"You little brats!" the statue yelled. "Couldn't you have been more careful? I mean, I'm more than three hundred years old!"

He shook his head angrily. I was afraid to move. How could a statue talk to us?

"Of course, I owe you two young men a lot for pulling me out of that cold, wet river," the statue added, more quietly. "But still. I'm very old. I can't take this kind of stress."

Lionel whispered, "What is going on?"

The statue ignored him and said, "Now, please help me climb up the hill. Then you'll have to carry me back to the city, where I have wanted to go for 312 years."

"Why?" Lionel asked. His voice shook.

"I have an important appointment," the statue said. "Now, if you don't mind, we'll have to hurry. I don't want to be late."

He stretched his tiny little hand toward us.

Lionel and I looked at each other. Then we walked down to the statue. When I grabbed the statue's hand, it was freezing cold.

Chapter 3

ARCHIBALD

I was glad we didn't pass anyone as we walked to the city that afternoon. If someone had walked nearby, they would have had a heart attack! After all, we were with a walking, talking statue.

When the statue walked, he was very slow. He made faces, and he sounded like screeching metal with each step. And he didn't stop talking the whole time. I think he was making up for being silent for 312 years.

His voice was very deep. It sounded like it was echoing from inside a large metal box.

The first thing the statue told us was his name. He said he was a statue made to look like Archibald Henning, a great astronomer from the 18th century. So that meant that the statue's name was Archibald.

An artist named Theo Brunitz had sculpted him more than three hundred years ago. Then the statue was sent on a boat to my city.

Unfortunately, the ship had sunk before it made it to my city. The whole crew had drowned, and everything on the ship was lost forever. No one knew what had happened to Archibald.

Archibald had sunk to the bottom of the river. He thought he would be rescued soon, but he was not.

Over a few hundred years, the river had slowly changed.

First, Archibald's fingers stuck out of the water. Then his arm did. Then Lionel and I found him and saved him.

Lionel and I listened to every word Archibald said. We believed him! We had dug him out, after all, and now he was walking next to us.

"So where are you going now?" Lionel asked.

Archibald lowered his voice and said, "Zelly is waiting for me."

"Who is Zelly?" I asked.

Archibald sighed. "Zelly is the moon of my nights, the sun of my days! During those years beneath the river, I could tell that she knew I was nearby!" he told us. Then he cried, "Wait for me, Zelly!"

I looked over at Lionel. He raised his eyebrows. I knew what he was thinking. He was thinking that Archibald really was crazy. I was starting to think that too.

I looked back at Archibald. "So, where is this Zelly person waiting for you?" I asked.

Archibald smiled. "Beautiful Zelly. She is being patient at the theater's front steps," he said. "I will meet her there."

Lionel stopped walking. "The theater?" he asked loudly. "It's all the way on the other side of town! No way. That will take way too long."

Lionel paused. Then he added, "Plus, how do you even know she's waiting for you? For all you know, she gave up. She doesn't think you're coming. I bet she gave up about a hundred years ago and left."

Archibald stopped smiling. He looked at Lionel angrily.

"Zelly is waiting for me! I know it and I feel it! She's been waiting for three hundred years now!" Archibald yelled.

He glared at Lionel. Then he went on, "And stop thinking that I'm crazy. Go wash your feet instead. They smell like you've been walking around in a cow pasture!"

Lionel and I looked at each other. How did Archibald know that we thought he was crazy?

Then I looked at Lionel's feet. His shoes were on. How did the statue know that Lionel's feet were stinky?

I thought for a minute. I had to figure out some way to make both of them happy. Otherwise, they'd drive me crazy too!

"The train station isn't far," I suggested. "We could take the train. It would be faster and way easier to get downtown on the train. Then, when we get to the city, we could carry you. Or we could pretend you were our little brother or something. We could pretend you were wearing a costume."

Archibald looked shocked. "Little brother?" he repeated. "Let me remind you that I am three centuries old, Samuel! Anyway, don't worry about that. I have friends in the city, and they know I'm coming back!"

"Yeah right!" Lionel muttered.

Archibald frowned. He said, "I think the person with stinky feet should have more trust in someone who is three hundred years older than he is!"

Neither of them said anything else until we got to the train station. Lionel didn't take any more pictures, either. I think he was upset.

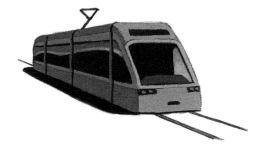

Chapter 4

FROZEN

"Hey, let me see your camera!"

We turned around. The boy who yelled at Lionel was standing in the aisle of the train with two other boys. Lionel, Archibald, and I were sitting in the back of the train, trying to stay out of sight, but the three boys had spotted us.

The tallest boy walked up to us. His two friends stood right behind him, blocking the way.

"Come on. Show me the camera," the boy said.

"No way. It's mine," Lionel told him.

"I don't care," the boy said. "So what if it's yours? Who's going to stop me? Your little friend here?" He pointed at me.

Then he looked at Archibald and laughed. "Or this little baby, wearing his little Halloween costume?" the boy added.

Then the boy grabbed the camera strap around Lionel's neck and pulled. He was trying to get the camera.

Lionel pulled too, trying to get away, but that just made things get even worse.

The boy kept pulling. He almost strangled Lionel!

Without thinking, I jumped up over the seat to help Lionel. But the bully pushed me, and I fell down between two seats.

Then Archibald stood up as tall as he could, which really wasn't very tall at all. In a deep voice, he yelled, "You! The good-for-nothing boy with yellow teeth. You must let go of this child right away, or else!"

The boy laughed and turned around. "Are you talking to me, little boy?" the bully asked.

"Yes, you," Archibald said. "The one with yellow teeth and monkey breath!"

The boy walked toward Archibald, making a fist. Archibald didn't let him get any closer.

The statue pointed his little finger at the bully. The boy froze in the middle of the aisle, with one hand on the camera strap, and the other ready to slap Archibald.

Then Archibald pointed at the other two boys in the aisle and did the same thing to them.

The three boys stood, frozen, in the aisle of the train. Archibald sat back down in his seat.

"Remind me to free them when we get to town," he said calmly.

When he saw how shocked Lionel and I were, Archibald added, "Don't worry. They won't remember a thing!"

We got off the train soon. Then we started walking again.

The theater was all the way downtown. It was just past the public library. Normally, getting to the theater would take Lionel and me about ten minutes. We wouldn't think anything of it.

But Archibald was getting tired after our long hike. He kept wanting to stop and rest, and he wasn't talking very much.

Lionel and I were worried that if we carried Archibald, people would think we'd stolen the statue. So we just tried to walk slowly.

At the park, we stopped next to the fountain for a rest. A boy our age walked over to us. He looked into Archibald's eyes.

"Wow, your little statue is super cool!" the boy said. "What video game is it from? It looks like it's from a movie or something. I bet it was expensive. Where did you buy it?" he asked me. "Do you think they have any more like it? I really want one!"

"This is Archie, and we're trying to find Zelly," I told him, winking at Lionel. "Don't you know Archie and Zelly? Zelly is really hard to find," I added. "We've been looking all day!"

"Oh yeah, I played that before on my computer!" the boy lied. "It was awesome. I'm really good at it. I found Zelly in no time at all."

I laughed. The boy was just trying to act cool. He just kept staring at Archibald.

Then I turned to look at Archibald too. The statue was breathing so loudly. I was afraid he would die.

It sounds crazy to say that I was afraid a bronze statue would die, but that's exactly how I felt.

I started to really worry about my small statue friend.

Archibald was so out of breath that he could hardly talk. "Zelly is so close, Samuel! I can feel it!" he said, panting. "But I can't go any farther! I need your help, and help from my friends . . . maybe . . ."

"What should we do?" I asked.

"Look," Archibald said quietly. "And please listen carefully to my friend's advice!"

I didn't really understand what he meant at first.

Then I noticed that the boy who had been looking at Archibald was frozen nearby, just like the boys on the train had been.

Then I heard a lady's voice say, "He told you to hurry, Samuel. We will not be able to freeze the whole downtown very long!"

I turned around to see who'd spoken to me. Behind me, the tall fountain statue was smiling.

"Hurry up!" the statue repeated. "You must get Archibald to the theater as quickly as you can! We don't have much time! Hurry, Samuel, hurry!"

Everything in the city was frozen and still. Cars were stopped in the street. Right in front of me, a bus was stopped with frozen passengers inside.

People had been walking around on the sidewalk. They were frozen. People sitting on benches in the park were frozen. All of them had turned into statues!

"Wow!" Lionel yelled. "This is crazy! Hold on, Sam. I have to take some pictures!"

I shook my head. "There's no time!" I said. "You heard what the fountain lady said. Come on. Pick up Archibald's feet. Hurry!"

We picked up Archibald and started walking.

It was strange to walk through the city while everyone was frozen.

Customers were stopped in the stores. Some people were paralyzed in weird positions on the sidewalk.

Even the birds had stopped. They were stuck in the middle of the air.

But the strangest part was that the real statues, the ones made of stone, marble, or granite, had become alive! They were moving around, talking to each other, and calling to us from the buildings or stands they sat on.

"Come on, boys, you can do it!" they yelled. "Hurry up! Go as quickly as you can! We can't hold the spell much longer!"

We were going as fast as we could.

Archibald was heavy. It was hard to hurry.

Soon we walked past the big statue of our town's hero, General Cober.

As we passed the general, Archibald whispered, "She's there, General Cober, isn't she?"

The general nodded and smiled. "Of course. At the end of the street, my friend," he said. "Zelly has always been waiting for you!" He pointed his sword at the theater.

"Sam, I must be dreaming," Lionel said quietly.

"I don't think so," I said. "Come on, we're almost there."

It was hard work, but we kept going.

"I can see her!" I shouted suddenly. "In the middle of the square. There! It has to be her!"

"It is her!" Archibald whispered. I think I saw his small eyes light up.

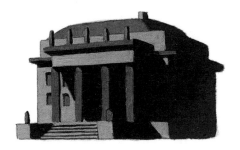

Chapter 5

ZELLY

She was meant for him, and he was meant for her!

They were the same size, made out of the same bronze. The same person had made them.

They were perfect together. You could tell that Archibald was meant to be right next to Zelly.

"We made it!" Lionel yelled.

I expected Archibald to say something, but the statue was silent. He just stared up at Zelly.

"Let's pick him up," I whispered to Lionel. "He should stand next to Zelly. That's where he belongs."

As we placed him next to her, Zelly turned her head to look at Archibald. She smiled. Archibald smiled back. I realized then that I had never seen him smile until that moment.

Archibald looked at Lionel and me. "Zelly was on a different boat," he whispered to us. "She arrived three months before my boat was supposed to get here. I always knew she was waiting for me!"

A real, wet tear slid down Archibald's smooth bronze face. Then he stretched his left arm out and carefully put it around Zelly's waist.

He lifted his right arm toward the sky, as if he was pointing at a star. Zelly raised her pretty face to look where he was pointing.

Finally, they froze in that position, together at last.

"Hey, Archibald!" Lionel said. "Look at me. I want to take your picture. Look this way!"

But the double statue did not move at all.

"Archibald? Miss Zelly?" Lionel whispered. "Just one little picture, please?"

Around us, I noticed that life had gone back to normal. The cars were rolling, and the walkers were walking. The birds were flying in the sky, and the statues were all quiet again. And Archibald and Zelly were quiet too.

I put my hand on my friend's shoulder. "Leave them alone, Lionel," I said quietly. "They are finally together. They're not going to move anymore."

* * *

No one could explain how the new statue had joined the lonely one by the theater.

In fact, the mayor offered a special gold medal to whoever had donated the statue, if the person would tell the city who they were. But of course, no one did.

No one knew the truth except me, Lionel, and all of the statues.

"We should go see the mayor and show him my picture," Lionel said, waving the picture I had taken of him with Archibald.

But I thought he was wrong. "Leave Archibald's mystery to himself," I said. "That's how it's supposed to be."

I know I'm right. Every time I go for a walk in the square by the theater, Zelly and Archie slowly turn their heads and smile at me.

When I walk by General Cober or the seated lady in the fountain, I hear them greet me.

They whisper, "Hello, little boy who saved Archibald!"

It always makes me smile. I wonder if people think I'm strange when I smile at the statues.

THE END

ABOUT THE AUTHOR

Hubert Ben Kemoun was born in 1958 in
Algeria, on the northern coast of Africa. He
has written plays for radio, screenplays for
television, musicals for the stage, and children's
books. He now lives in Nantes, France, with his
wife and their two sons, Nicolas and Nathan.
He likes writing detective stories, and also creates
crossword puzzles for newspapers. When he
writes stories, he writes them first with a pen
and then copies the words onto a computer.
His favorite color is black, the color of ink.

ABOUT THE ILLUSTRATOR

Thomas Ehretsmann was born in 1974 on the
eastern border of France in the town of Mulhouse
(pronounced mee-yoo-looz). He created his own
comic strips at the age of 6, inspired by the
newspapers his father read. Ehretsmann studied
decorative arts in the ancient cathedral town of
Strassbourg, and worked with a world-famous
publisher of graphic novels, Delcourt Editions.
Ehretsmann now works primarily as an
illustrator of books for adults and children.

GLOSSARY

appointment (uh-POINT-muhnt)—a planned meeting

astronomer (uh-STRON-uh-mur)—someone who studies planets, stars, and space

balance (BAL-uhnss)—the ability to not fall over

bronze (BRONZ)—a hard, reddish-brown metal that is a mixture of copper and tin

century (SEN-chur-ee)—one hundred years

expensive (ek-SPEN-siv)—costing a lot of money

paralyzed (PA-ruh-lized)—helpless or unable to move

pasture (PASS-chur)—grazing land for animals

patient (PAY-shuhnt)—good at waiting calmly

sculpted (SKUHLPT-id)—carved or shaped out of stone, wood, metal, marble, or clay

square (SKWAIR)—an open area in a town or city with streets on all four sides

statue (STACH-oo)—a model of a person or an animal made from a solid material

strangled (STRANG-guhld)—choked

treasure (TREZH-ur)—something valuable that has been found

FAMOUS STATUES

Statues are found in cultures throughout the world. Some mark events in history. Some recognize important people. And some come from an artist's imagination. Here are some of the world's most famous statues:

Rio de Janeiro, Brazil is known for its towering statue, **Christ the Redeemer**. It stands 2,430 feet (741 meters) tall on Corcovado Mountain. Completed in 1931, 300,000 people from all over the world visit it each year. A twenty-minute train ride carries visitors to the statue's base.

The **Great Sphinx of Giza** was built as a pharaoh's temple in Egypt 4,500 years ago. The sphinx is a half-lion, half human figure. It is the largest stone statue in the world, measuring 240 feet (73 meters) long and 66 feet (20 meters) high.

FROM AROUND THE WORLD

Standing nearly 17 feet (5 meters) tall, the **Statue of David** is made of Italian marble. The statue was started by artist Donatello, who died shortly after beginning. The project was stalled for 25 years before Michelangelo took over. He completed it three years later, in 1504.

At 152 feet (46.4 meters), the **Statue of Liberty** in New York is the tallest gift the United States has ever received. France gave the copper statue as a symbol of international friendship. It was first built in France. It was then broken apart into 350 pieces, then packed into 214 crates for its journey to the United States.

DISCUSSION QUESTIONS

1. Archibald and Zelly are statues. Talk about other statues you have seen or read about. What else do you know about statues?

2. On the train, Archibald froze the bullies. What were some other ways that Sam and Lionel could have handled the problem?

3. At the end of this book, Sam doesn't want to tell anyone where Archibald came from. Why? What would you do? Talk about your answers.

WRITING PROMPTS

1. Pretend that the statues have frozen everything in your town or city — except for you and your best friend. What would you do? Where would you go? Write about how you would spend a day when everything else was frozen.

2. In this book, a statue comes to life. Choose a piece of art and pretend that it came to life. Write about what the piece of art might say.

3. Sam and Lionel are best friends who do almost everything together. Write about your best friend. What do you like to do together? What do you like about your friend?

More Sam X Adventures!

The Adventures of Sam X

Whimsical, colorful, and intense, these chapter books follow the surreal life of Sam X. Join Sam X and his best friend, Lionel, as they embark on strange adventures — controlling the weather, losing a shadow, and watching a snake tattoo come to life!

Visit www.stonearchbooks.com

INTERNET SITES

Do you want to know more about subjects related to this book? Or are you interested in learning about other topics? Then check out FactHound, a fun, easy way to find Internet sites.

Our investigative staff has already sniffed out great sites for you!

Here's how to use FactHound:

1. Visit *www.facthound.com*

2. Select your grade level.

3. To learn more about subjects related to this book, type in the book's ISBN number: **9781434212207**.

4. Click the **Fetch It** button.

FactHound will fetch the best Internet sites for you!